For Lucy, Joseph, and William —A. McA.

For Heidi. It's good to have you home! —D. H.

Text copyright © 2008 by Angela McAllister
Illustrations copyright © 2008 by Daniel Howarth
First published in Great Britain in 2008 by Gullane Children's Books.

Library of Congress Cataloging-in-Publication Data
McAllister, Angela.
Santa's little helper / Angela McAllister ; [illustrations by] Daniel Howarth — 1st Orchard Books ed. p. cm.
Summary: During a game of hide-and-seek Snowball, an arctic hare, hides in Santa's sleigh
and when Santa Claus finds him, Santa requests his help to deliver presents.
ISBN-13: 978-0-545-09444-3 (reinforced lib. bdg.)
ISBN-10: 0-545-09444-5 (reinforced lib. bdg.)
[1. Arctic hare–Fiction. 2. Hares–Fiction 3. Helpfulness–Fiction. 4.Christmas–Fiction.] I. Howarth, Daniel, ill. II.
Title. PZ7.M47825San 2008 [E]–dc22

10 9 8 7 6 5 4 3 2   08 09 10 11 12

Printed in Indonesia
Reinforced Binding for Library Use
First edition, October 2008

Santa's Little Helper

By Angela McAllister · Illustrated by Daniel Howarth

ORCHARD BOOKS · NEW YORK
An Imprint of Scholastic, Inc.

It was the day before Christmas.
Snowball was excited.
He hopped and skipped to play with his
brothers and sisters.

He hurried past his friends building a snowman.

He giggled at Mr. Polar Bear's stories.

Soon he met his brothers and sisters.
"We are going to play hide-and-seek!" they yelled.
"Do you want to play?"
"Yes," said Snowball, and he set off to
find a good place to hide.

The first place wasn't
big enough.
So he went farther.

"Can I hide behind you?"
Snowball asked Mr. Walrus.
"Sorry, Snowball," he replied.
"I was just going swimming."

The next place Snowball
found was too cozy.

So he kept looking.

Snowball was so excited.
He had found a perfect place to hide.
He stayed very still.

He waited and waited and waited and waited.
But nobody could find him.
Snowball was so quiet that, after a while, he fell asleep.

Snowball didn't hear the footsteps crunching through the snow.
"Ho! Ho! Ho!" a voice chuckled. "I nearly left this behind."
Santa picked up the sleeping bunny and
placed him in his sack of presents.

Snowball woke to the sound of jingle bells and
a deep voice humming a merry tune.

Snowball peeped out.
The starry sky spun around him.
The wind whistled through his whiskers.
"I must be dreaming!" he gasped.

Then the sleigh landed with
a bump . . . and Snowball tumbled
out into the snow!

"Hello there, little one," chuckled Santa Claus. He picked Snowball up.
"What a surprise! I thought you were one of the toys!"

"Would you be my little helper?" he asked.
Snowball nodded happily.

There were stockings to fill.

There was so much to be done.

There were lots of presents to carry.

At last all the sacks were empty.
"Merry Christmas, Snowball," said Santa Claus.
"I could never have done all this without you."
Then he gave Snowball a special Christmas present.
"Now we'd better get you home!" he smiled.

Santa tucked Snowball under
a warm, cozy blanket and he fell asleep.
The reindeer galloped through the night sky.

Snowball didn't even wake up when Santa Claus carried him back to his burrow.

The next morning his brothers and sisters found him at last.
"Where did you hide?" they asked. "We looked everywhere."
"I was so still and so quiet I fell asleep," said Snowball with a yawn.
"But I had a wonderful dream!"

"Well, you won't have to be still and quiet today," said his brothers and sisters.
"Come on! It's Christmas."
"Hurray!" cried Snowball. And, as he ran happily after them through the snow,
the jingle of a tiny bell told him that his Christmas dream was true!